P9-ECO-300

bark!
bark!

bark!

For my brave girl, Romy

ACKNOWLEDGMENTS

Thank you so much to everyone who helped make this book what it is, including Liz Szabla, Rich Deas, Jean Feiwel, Rosemary Stimola, Miriam Busch, Stacy Curtis, Larry Day, Candace Fleming, Julie Halpern, Edward Hemingway, Tom Lichtenheld, Mike Petrik, Eric Rohmann, Chris Sheban, Ed Spicer, Erin Stead, Philip Stead, and Mark Winter. Special thanks to Kira Cassidy of the Yellowstone Wolf Project for taking the time to answer in depth my questions about wolves and wolf behavior.

A FEIWEL AND FRIENDS BOOK
An Imprint of Macmillan

Printed in the United States of America by Worzalla, Stevens Point, Wisconsin.
For information, address Feiwel and Friends, 175 Fifth Avenue, New York, N.Y. 10010.

Our books may be purchased in bulk for promotional, educational, or business use. Please contact your local bookseller or the Macmillan Corporate and Premium Sales Department at (800) 221-7945 ext. 5442 or by e-mail at MacmillanSpecialMarkets@macmillan.com.

Library of Congress Control Number: 2016937562

ISBN: 978-1-250-07636-6

Book design by Eileen Gilshian

Feiwel and Friends logo designed by Filomena Tuosto

First Edition: 2017

5 7 9 10 8 6 4

The artwork was created with pen and ink with watercolor.

mackids.com

WOLF IN THE SNOW

Matthew Cordell

Feiwel and Friends
New York

SCHOOL

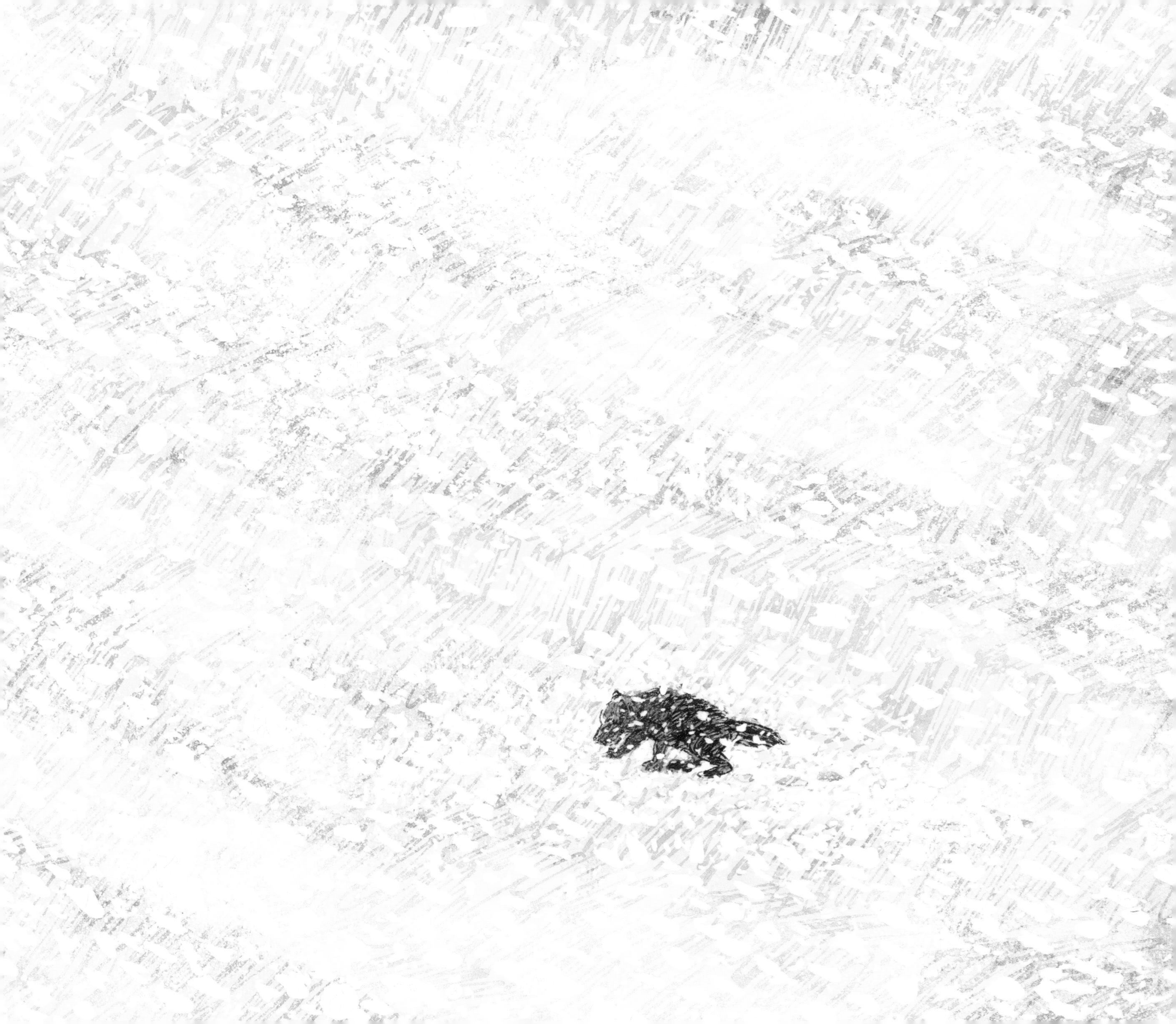

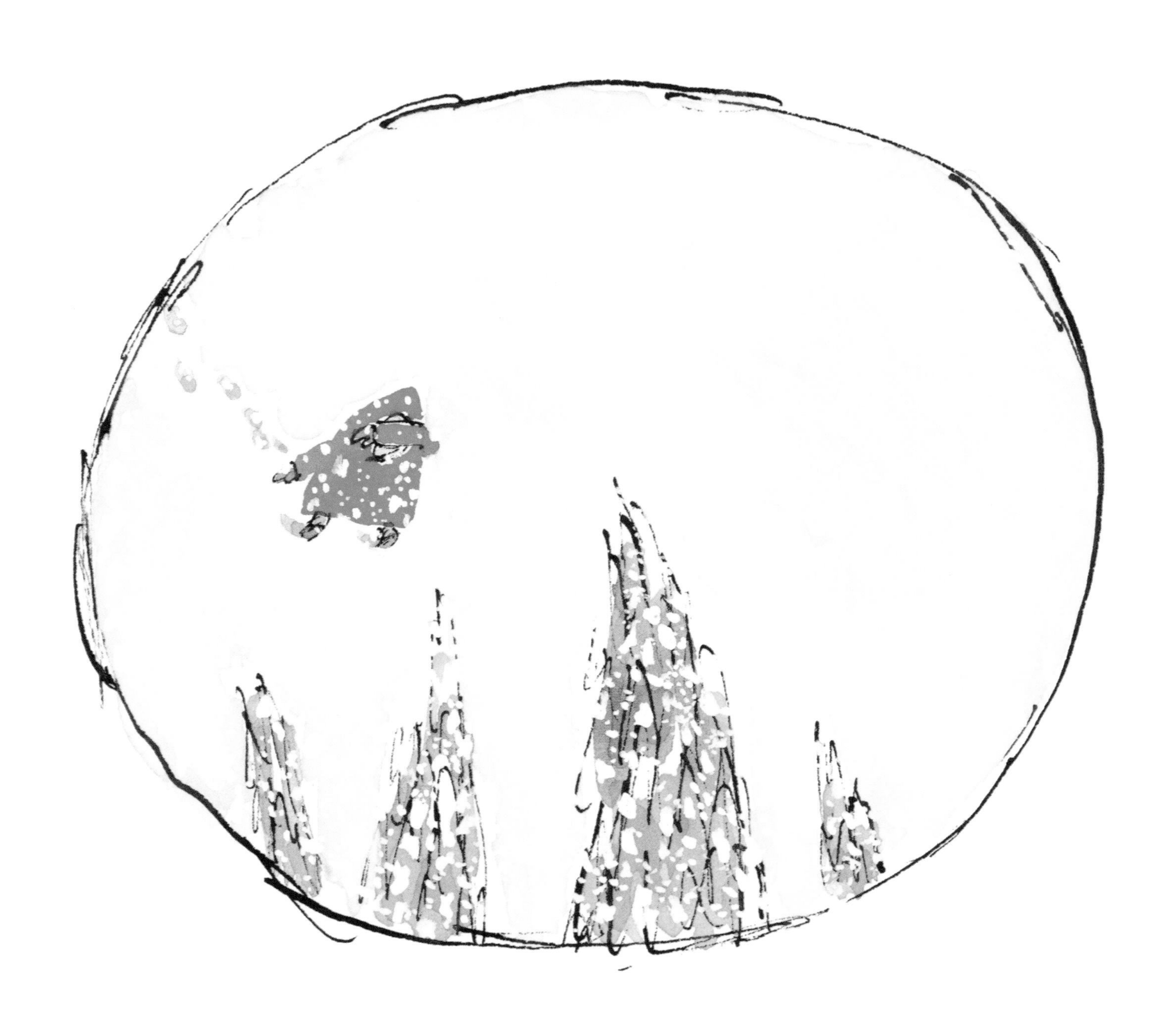

huff
huff

whine
whine

whine
whine
whine

sink!
whine
whine

howwll

?....
hoooooooooooooooooowww!!!!!

hoooooo oooooooowwwl

hoooooooooowwlll
GROWWLLL...

SCREECH!

HOOOOOOWWLLL

HOOWWWLL
huff huff

RRRRRRR

sink!
SNIFF!
lick lick

bark!
bark!

huff... huff...

bark!
bark!

bark!
lick-lick...

HOOOWWL
bark!
bark!

BARK!
BARK!

HOOOOOWWLLLL!!